HANS CHRISTIAN ANDERSEN

Thumbelina

RETOLD BY DEBORAH HAUTZIG · ILLUSTRATED BY KAARINA KAILA

Alfred A. Knopf New York

There was once a woman who wanted to have a child of her own, but she had no idea where to get one. So she went to ask an old witch.

"A child?" said the witch. "Nothing is easier! Take this magic barleycorn. Put it in a flowerpot and see what happens!"

The woman planted the barleycorn, and in no time a lovely tulip came up. "How beautiful!" said the woman. She kissed the closed petals. Instantly the flower burst open. And sitting in the center was a tiny little girl. She was so delicate and pretty! And she was no taller than your thumb. So she was given the name Thumbelina.

At night Thumbelina slept in a walnut shell. Her mattress was made of blue violet petals, and a rose leaf was her blanket. In the daytime Thumbelina played about on a table where the woman had put a dish of flowers. Thumbelina liked to sit on a tulip leaf and row from one side of the dish to the other, using white horsehairs as oars. She often sang as she rowed about, and she had the sweetest voice anyone had ever heard.

One night, as Thumbelina slept, an ugly toad hopped through the window and landed beside her cradle.

"She would make such a nice wife for my son!" thought the toad. She snatched the sleeping Thumbelina and hopped out the window into the garden.

"Ribbet! Ribbet!" said the toad's son when he saw Thumbelina. He was slimy and horrible—just like his mother. The toads put Thumbelina on a water-lily leaf in the middle of the garden brook so that she couldn't escape.

When Thumbelina woke up and saw where she was, she cried bitterly. The toads swam to the lily leaf.

"Why are you crying, silly girl? You will have a lovely home with my son, under the mud!" said the old mother toad. Then the toads swam back to shore to prepare for the wedding.

Thumbelina sat all alone and cried. She didn't want to marry the horrible toad! What was she going to do?

The fish swimming in the brook heard what the awful toad said, and they heard Thumbelina crying. They wanted to help her, so they nibbled away at the stalk beneath the water-lily leaf. The leaf floated away with Thumbelina, far away where the toads could never reach her.

Thumbelina went sailing past all sorts of beautiful places, and birds sang to her as she passed. The sunshine gleamed on the water like the finest gold.

Suddenly a large beetle came flying over. When he saw Thumbelina, he clutched her round the waist and flew with her over the meadow and up into a tree. "How pretty you are!" he said. "Though you're not a bit like a beetle." Later, all the beetles who lived in the tree came to visit. "She's only got two legs!" they exclaimed. "She has no feelers! Oh, how ugly she is!"

Thumbelina wasn't ugly at all, of course, and the beetle who had carried her knew this. But as the others kept saying she was ugly, the beetle began to think so too. He wanted nothing to do with her. So Thumbelina was left alone again. She cried because she was so ugly that even the beetles didn't want her. And all the time she was as beautiful as could be.

Right through the summer and autumn, Thumbelina lived in that enormous meadow. She took blades of grass and braided them to make a bed. She got her food from the honey in the flowers and her drink from the morning dew on the leaves.

But then winter came. All the birds that had sung to her flew away. The trees and flowers withered, and snow began to fall. By now, Thumbelina's dress was thin and tattered. She wrapped herself in a dead leaf and shivered with cold.

One day, as she walked through a frozen field, she came to a field mouse's door. It was a little hole below the stubble. Thumbelina went in and asked for a bit of barleycorn.

"You poor thing!" said the kind old field mouse. "Come eat with me in my warm room." The mouse liked Thumbelina right away and said she could stay for the winter, if she promised to tell lots of stories. Thumbelina stayed with the mouse, and she was very comfortable.

"My neighbor, the mole, is coming to visit," the mouse said one day. "His house is even nicer than mine. He doesn't see well, but he's very rich and clever. He would be a wonderful husband for you!"

The mole was indeed clever. He knew a great many things. But he couldn't bear sunshine and pretty flowers, and he said nasty things about them even though he'd never really seen them.

The mole had dug a long tunnel through the earth, leading from his house to where Thumbelina lived with the field mouse. The three of them went strolling in this tunnel. It was dark, but the mole held a small light so the mouse and Thumbelina could find their way. Soon they came to where a dead bird was lying. "Don't be afraid," said the mole. "The bird died when winter began." The mole tilted his snout up to the ceiling and thrust it through the earth. Now there was a large hole, and sunlight poured into the tunnel.

Thumbelina could see the dead swallow with its pretty wings folded close to its sides. She felt so sorry for it!

The mole kicked at the bird, saying, "How awful to be born a bird! It does nothing but sing, and then starve to death when winter comes."

"Yes, starve and freeze. Oh, you are so sensible," said the field mouse.

Thumbelina said nothing.

When the mole and the field mouse turned their backs on the bird, Thumbelina stooped down. She smoothed aside the feathers that lay over the bird's head and kissed its closed eyes.

That night Thumbelina couldn't sleep. She got up and carried a blanket to the dead bird. She spread it over him, tucking bits of cotton from the field mouse's sewing basket at the sides so the bird could be warm in the cold earth. "Good-bye, bird," she whispered. She laid her head against the bird's breast. And what a fright she had! She heard a thumping sound inside. It was the bird's heart. He wasn't dead at all! As the bird grew warmer he began to wake up. Thumbelina trembled, but she tried not to be afraid.

"Thank you, my dear child," said the swallow. "I'm warmer now."

The swallow stayed all winter, and Thumbelina took care of him. He told her how he had torn his wing on a bramble and couldn't keep up with the other swallows when they flew away to the warm countries.

Spring arrived, and the sun began to warm the earth. It was time for the swallow to leave.

"Wouldn't you like to come with me?" asked the swallow. "You could sit on my back and we would fly to the beautiful green forest."

Thumbelina did want to go! But she knew how sad the field mouse would be if she left so suddenly. So she said, "I'm sorry, but I can't."

"Good-bye then, you dear, kind girl," said the swallow, and he flew off into the sunshine. Thumbelina loved the swallow and waved good-bye to him with tears in her eyes.

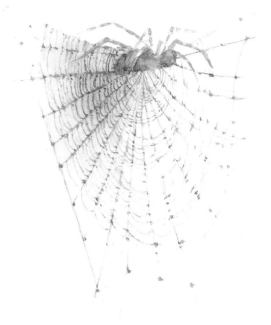

Thumbelina spent the spring underground, and it made her very sad. She was never allowed to go out in the sunshine, and to make matters worse, the tiresome old mole had proposed marriage to her.

"You have to prepare for your wedding," the mouse told her. "You'll need woolens and linen for your trousseau."

Thumbelina wept. She didn't want to marry the mole! But the mouse said, "Don't be so pigheaded. He'll make a splendid husband! Stop this nonsense."

So Thumbelina spun wool and linen, and the field mouse asked four spiders to weave day and night. The mole visited every evening. He talked about how wonderful it would be when summer was over and the earth grew cold and dark again. Thumbelina thought the mole was gloomy and a terrible bore. Every morning she gazed out the door at the blue sky and thought how dazzling it was out there. She wished she could see the swallow once more!

Summer ended and the wedding day arrived. The mole was ready to take Thumbelina deep under the earth, where she would never again see the sun shine.

Thumbelina stepped outside the field mouse's house and threw her tiny arms around a little red flower. "Good-bye, sun!" she said sadly. "Good-bye, flower. Remember me to the dear swallow, if you happen to see him!"

Suddenly she heard a familiar voice. She looked up, and there was the swallow. He was so happy to see her! Thumbelina told the swallow all about having to marry the dreadful mole, and she began to cry.

"Will you come with me now?" asked the swallow. "We'll fly far away from the gloomy mole to the warm countries, where it's always summer. Dear Thumbelina, you saved my life. Now let me help you. Will you come?"

Thumbelina stopped crying. She smiled and said, "Yes. I'll come!"

Thumbelina climbed onto the bird's back. She tied her sash to one of the strongest feathers. Then the swallow flew high into the air. They soared over lakes and forests and great mountains.

At last they reached the warm countries. Thumbelina had never seen the sun shine so brightly! On the slopes grew the finest grapes, and lemons and oranges hung from the trees. The lakes were sapphire blue. The air smelled sweetly of myrtle and curled mint, and butterflies played among the flowers. The swallow came to a nest atop a glittering white marble palace.

"Here's my house!" said the swallow to Thumbelina. "But you see those flowers down there? You can choose one and I'll put you on it. It will be a cozy home for you."

The swallow placed Thumbelina on a broad white petal. But what a surprise she had! There in the middle of the flower sat a tiny man. He shimmered as if he were made of glass. He wore a little gold crown on his head and the most exquisite wings on his shoulders. And he was no bigger than Thumbelina!

The tiny man was the guardian spirit of the flower. Each flower had just such a man or lady living in it. But this one was King of them all.

"How handsome he is!" whispered Thumbelina to the swallow.

When the man saw Thumbelina, he was enchanted. He took the gold crown off his head and placed it on hers. Then he said, "Will you be my wife and become Queen of all flowers?"

Thumbelina thought the kind, handsome King would make a wonderful husband for her! So she said, "Yes, I will."

All the birds sang for them in celebration. From every flower there appeared a dapper little lady or gentleman, and each brought a present for Thumbelina. The best present of all was a pair of beautiful wings, which were fastened to her back. The swallow sat up in his nest and smiled as he watched Thumbelina fly from flower to flower. She was finally happy.

And that is how Thumbelina became the guardian spirit Queen of flowers, as gentle and lovely as the day she was born.